THIS WALKER BOOK BELONGS TO:

_____

_____

_____

_____

First published 1984 by Walker Books Ltd
87 Vauxhall Walk, London SE11 5HJ
as *The Building Site*

This edition published 1994
© 1984 Philippe Dupasquier

Printed and bound in Hong Kong
by Sheck Wah Tong Printing Press Ltd

British Library Cataloguing in Publication Data
A catalogue record for this book is
available from the British Library.

ISBN 0-7445-3138-1

A Busy Day at the Building Site

PHILIPPE DUPASQUIER

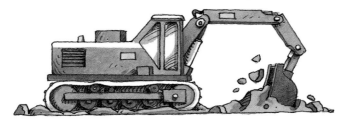

WALKER BOOKS
LONDON

It is early morning.

The building site is quiet.

Nothing disturbs Old Sam or his dog Tinker.

The works van arrives.

"Let's have no dawdling about now, lads,"

says J.K. Biggs, the foreman, to his men.

Aaah! Oooh!

Old Sam and Tinker stretch and yawn.

Scrunch! Scrape! The digger starts to dig.

Rumble! Slurp! The cement truck mixes and pours.

"This way a bit!" Eddie shouts to the crane driver.

"I've told you before to stay off the site,"
says J.K. Biggs to Old Sam. "Just don't
come back again, you hear!"

Roar! Clatter! The bulldozer crawls in.
Eddie and Pat direct the crane.

"Just get those bricks laid as quickly as
you can," says J.K. Biggs to Micky,
the bricklayer, and Ben, his mate.

Thump! Crash! The bulldozer loads
the tip-up truck, while the driver has a chat.

"Hey, Ben, watch that hook!"
Micky calls down, above all the noise.

The surveyor and the architect drive in,
and carefully discuss the plans.

"Help!" yells J.K. Biggs,
suddenly lifted up into the air.

"Bring it straight in!" shouts Jim,
directing the low-loader.

"I've never had such a shock in my life,"
says J.K. Biggs, all white and trembling.

"Straight up! Right a bit! OK!" Jim
shouts, as the crane lifts the girders
off the low-loader.

Up on the platform everyone stops to watch.
"Not much longer," thinks J.K. Biggs,
checking the time.

The works van comes to collect the men,
to take them all home.

Two familiar faces watch them go.

The day is over. The site is quiet again.

Old Sam and Tinker make themselves at home.

MORE WALKER PAPERBACKS
For You to Enjoy

Also by Philippe Dupasquier

BUSY DAYS

There are six books in this series – all of them full of things to spot and enjoy.

*"The balance of continuity and change is beautifully even,
the illustrations are bright, full of detail but never confusing, and
the books are, above all, fun."* British Book News

0-7445-3135-7   *A Busy Day at the Railway Station*
0-7445-3140-3   *A Busy Day at the Factory*
0-7445-3137-3   *A Busy Day at the Harbour*
0-7445-3136-5   *A Busy Day at the Garage*
0-7445-3139-X   *A Busy Day at the Airport*
0-7445-3138-1   *A Busy Day at the Building Site*
£3.99 each

I CAN'T SLEEP

The story of one family's sleepless night.

"This wordless story is full of wit, warmth and wonderful pictures."
Tony Bradman, Parents

0-7445-2061-4   £3.99

FOLLOW THAT CHIMP

When Chimp escapes from the zoo, his keepers follow him, and the
most amazing chase begins – across land, sea and air; on trains,
planes, cars and ships... But will Chimp get away? Look through
this wonderful comic-strip picture book and you'll find out!

0-7445-2511-X   £3.99

**Walker Paperbacks are available from most booksellers, or by post from
Walker Books Ltd, PO Box 11, Falmouth, Cornwall TR10 9EN.**

To order, send: Title, author, ISBN number and price for each book ordered, your full name and address, cheque or postal order
for the total amount, plus postage and packing: UK and BFPO Customers – £1.00 for first book, plus 50p for the second book and plus 30p
for each additional book to a maximum charge of £3.00. Overseas and Eire Customers – £2.00 for first book, plus £1.00 for the second book
and plus 50p per copy for each additional book. Prices are correct at time of going to press, but are subject to change without notice.